I hereby grant this book to:

....

(Make it snappy, would you?
I'm a busy woman.)

NOT

Just Another

PRINCESS

STORY

written by SHERI RADFORD
illustrated by QIN LENG

simply read books

To Paul. I had to kiss a lot of frogs
before I found you.
—SR

To my dearest sister Lian,
who will recognize herself in Candi.
—QL

Published in 2014 by Simply Read Books, *okay?* | www.simplyreadbooks.com
Text © 2014 Sheri Radford
Illustrations © 2014 Qin Leng

Library and Archives Canada Cataloguing in Publication
(This is the official stuff, okay?)

Radford, Sheri, 1971-, author
Not just another princess story / written by Sheri Radford
; illustrated by Qin Leng.
ISBN 978-1-927018-57-6 (bound)
I. Leng, Qin, illustrator II. Title.
PS8635.A337N68 2014   jC813'.6   C2014-900444-3

We gratefully acknowledge for their financial support of our publishing program the Canada Council for the Arts, the BC Arts Council, and the Government of Canada through the Canada Book Fund (CBF). *Thank you!*

Manufactured in Malaysia.
Book design by Heather Lohnes.

10 9 8 7 6 5 4 3 2 1

TABLE *of* CONTENTS

Math is boring!

I. THE BEGINNING
OF COURSE!

Once upon a time there was a princess named Princess Candi. Now, she was no ordinary princess. She was super-duper-extra beautiful and she was also super-duper-extra intelligent. Well, she was intelligent at least. Look, let's just say she wasn't totally stupid. *Okay?*

Candi was at least smart enough to know that not just any old prince was good enough for her, and certainly not any old prince that her father *(the king, of course)* chose for her. What did her father know about choosing princes? He'd never chosen one before. He hadn't even chosen Candi's mother, the queen. He'd won her in a high stakes poker game from a wizard who had already lost his watch, a faraway tract of swampland, a rather nice pair of silk boxer shorts, and all his oxen. Unfortunately for the king, the spiteful wizard turned the queen into a large pickle just after Candi was born. The king kept the queen in the pantry now, but she wasn't much company to anybody, being a pickle and all.

The wizard also placed a spell on the king that made the king a bit, well, silly. Everyone was much too polite to mention the change in the king, but they all noticed it—everyone, that

is, except Candi. As long as Candi had been alive the king had been rather, well, goofy, but Candi loved him just the same.

Loved him, but that didn't mean she trusted him to select a prince for her. The king had never even picked out a suit of clothing for himself, never mind a prince whom his daughter would have to love and cherish and *blah blah blah* for the rest of her life. The king relied on thousands of servants *(well, dozens, anyway)* to do boring stuff such as choose his clothes and cook food and start wars. His butterfly collection took up most of his time, but now that Candi was nineteen *(as one of his servants pointed out)*, he decided it was time to find her a husband.

"Daughter, we must talk," he announced one day. He always called her "Daughter" when he couldn't remember her name. He had called her "Fudge Nougat" once and "Jujube" another time, but fortunately Candi had misunderstood these as terms of affection. *(Hey, I said Candi was smart, not a genius. Okay?)*

"Yes, Father," Candi replied, putting down the book of mathematical problems that she had been working on. She found the logic of math soothing.

"It's time for you to get married," the king said.

"Okay," Candi said. *(Remember, this was once upon a time, which was a long time ago. It was a time when people did silly things such as obey their parents, get married really young, and eat Brussels sprouts as bedtime snacks.)* For three long days she thought about what her father had said, and finally she confronted him, quite distraught.

"Father, I am confused," she said.

"Why, er, Daughter?" the king asked, putting aside the

pretty pink and blue butterfly he was studying.

"It doesn't add up. How am I to be married without a prince? You need two people to get married, don't you?" she asked.

The king shook his head and wondered to himself for the billionth time *(or hundredth time, at least)* why he had a daughter instead of a dog, a nice cocker spaniel maybe, that would bring him his slippers and his pipe. *(If he smoked a pipe, that is.)* All his daughter brought him were headaches, along with an occasional slight cramping feeling in the bottom of his left foot. It wasn't fair to blame this cramping feeling on Candi, but the king went ahead and did so anyway.

"I will find you a prince, and then you can get married," the king explained in his best patient-and-loving-father voice.

Candi thought about what her father had said for another three days, and finally, quite distraught, she confronted him.

"Father, I am again confused," she said.

"Again, my little, er, Jelly Bean?"

"Yes. Why do you have to find me a prince? Why can't I find one for myself?"

"It's not tradition."

"So?"

The king was speechless for a minute. "Well, tradition is tradition," he finally said, hoping this brilliantly logical statement would satisfy his daughter, so that he could get back to the beautiful yellow and green butterfly he had been examining.

"So?"

Again the king was speechless.

"If I must get involved in this obtuse marriage business, I want at least to choose my future pickle for myself," Candi said.

"Not all spouses end up as pickles, my little Chocolate Bar."

This was news to Candi. "You mean," she said slowly, "that people get married and stay people?"

"Yes."

A puzzled expression crept across Candi's face. "And the man I marry, I will have to live with?"

"Forever."

Candi's puzzled expression looked like it might stick around for a while. "And he will not turn into a pickle?"

"Probably not."

Candi pondered this new information for a few moments and came to a decision. "Then I definitely want to find my prince, my husband, my non-pickle, for myself."

The king glanced longingly at the yellow and green butterfly before him and wished with all his might that his daughter would go away and do, well, something other than what she was presently doing. It occurred to him that if she were to find her own husband, it would occupy her for quite a while, which would give him more time to spend with his beloved butterflies.

"I have made a decision," he announced in what he hoped was a noble, kingly voice. "I am going to break with tradition and allow you to find your own husband."

Candi threw her arms around her father's neck. "Thank you!" she exclaimed.

The king smiled at his daughter and, untangling himself from her arms, turned back to his butterfly.

"That's a beautiful yellow and green butterfly, Father. What is it called?"

"A yellow and green butterfly, of course."

"How very logical." Candi carefully filed away this intriguing bit of information in her brain as she dashed off to her room. Finding a prince seemed so exciting that she skipped her daily three to four hours of math equations. She decided to get to work right away on this husband-finding business. That's when she realized that she didn't know anything about looking for a husband, or what to do with one if she found one.

Candi's father was a husband, and what did he do all day? He looked at pretty butterflies and occasionally crept into the kitchen to steal a taste of chocolate chip cookie batter while the cook wasn't looking. That was it. If that was all husbands did, Candi decided they were a pretty boring lot. She wanted to ask her father if husbands had any other purpose, but her father was a busy man, what with his butterflies and cookie batter and all, and she didn't want to bother him.

It was time for a mother-daughter talk. She had never had one of these before, but they were what always happened in the novels she read whenever she grew tired of doing math. She went to the pantry and found her mother.

"Mother," Candi said, "I need to find a husband but I don't know what to look for."

Her mother, being a large pickle, said nothing. Candi tried again.

"What kind of man could I live with forever? And how do

I find such a man?"

Candi's mother just sat and did, well, whatever it is that pickles do *(which isn't much beyond not move and be green)*.

"Pickle, pickle in the jar, how can I find husbands near and far?"

Still nothing. Candi felt very frustrated. "I'm very frustrated!" she said to her mother, before returning to her room. She sat on her bed and waited for inspiration to strike.

Three days later, it struck. Candi ran as fast as she could to the attic and searched for a certain box.

It took quite a while for her to find it *(castles have big attics, you know)* but eventually she did. It was labeled "Remnants of Candi's Childhood."

She tore it open and dug around until she found a large book of fairy tales. She opened the book and began reading. Four and a half hours later, she slammed shut the book with a triumphant bang.

"I have calculated how to find a husband!" she exclaimed as she ran downstairs. She found a piece of paper and wrote a list of four ways to find a husband. She pinned the list up on her wall, where she would see it when she woke up every morning. She decided to get started right away on method number one.

"Send all the princes in the area off to slay a dragon or a giant," Candi read from the list. "Whoever slays it is definitely husband material. You can count on it."

II. KILLING MONSTERS

ATTENTION ALL PRINCES!

ASSEMBLE AT THE PALACE TOMORROW AT 9:00 A.M. TO HEAR AN EXTREMELY IMPORTANT ANNOUNCEMENT

Candi made up dozens of bright, colorful posters. She hung the posters all over town, then went to tell her father about her plan. She found him in the kitchen, with his finger in a bowl of chocolate chip cookie batter.

"Father! I am so very excited!" she said.

"Oh, yes, hello, Daughter. I was just, er, overseeing the making of our dinner," the king said nervously, hiding his cookie-batter-covered finger behind his back.

"I have figured out how to find a husband."

"That is great news, truly splendid news. Now run along," the king said, licking his lips while staring at the cookie batter.

"I have placed posters all over town—"

"Splendid, splendid," the king interrupted. "When the police are looking for criminals, they put up posters. I'm sure you'll find a husband. Now run along, my little Gumdrop."

"You don't understand," Candi said, but the king wasn't listening. He was gazing longingly into the bowl of cookie batter. With a sigh, Candi left her father to his important business and returned to her room, where she could plan what to say in her Extremely Important Announcement.

The next morning, all the princes in the land were gathered in front of the castle.

"My dear princes," Candi began, "it is time for me to get married, and I must marry one of you."

The princes began running around in circles, slapping each other on the back and hooting while making armpit noises.

"Whoever is the first to slay a dragon or a monster will be my husband," Candi continued. The princes grew quiet.

"Are you crazy?" one of them finally shouted.

"That sounds dangerous!" another said.

"What do you think this is, a fairy tale?"

"Go kill your own monster, lady!"

"Where the heck are we going to find a monster around here?"

Some of the less brave princes began to cry. Candi knew she had to do something to regain control of the situation.

"I will also give my husband a bag of gold—the maximum

he can carry!" she cried. This caught the interest of the greedier princes, and off they went to kill some monsters.

Candi went back to her room and waited. After three days of waiting while nothing happened, she grew bored. She pulled out a brand new book of mathematical puzzles and set to work figuring them out. Solving the problems soothed her troubled mind.

After another three days, when she had pretty well given up hope on method number one of ways to find a husband, there was a great commotion outside the castle. Candi ran out to see what was going on. She pushed her way to the center of the thousands of people *(well, dozens, anyway)* who had gathered and saw one dead giant, two dead dragons, and three live princes. The princes, who were having a heated argument, all bowed down low when they saw Princess Candi.

"My most dear Princess, my love, my future wife," the first prince said.

"She's going to be my wife, bub!" the second prince shouted, shoving the first prince.

"Back off, Romeos! She's mine!" the third prince cried, giving the other two a push.

"What on earth is going on here?" Candi yelled above the noise.

"I killed this dragon, here," the first prince said, indicating the larger of the two dragons, "so I will be your husband, and—"

"Hey! I killed this dragon here," the second prince interrupted, pointing to the smaller of the two dragons, "so I will be your husband, and—"

"But I killed this monster," the third prince interrupted the interrupter, "so I'm really your husband-to-be."

Candi shook her head.

"This is all very confusing to me," she said. "Let me think about this and calculate what to do." She thought long and hard. She thought about all the fairy tales she had ever read, but they were no help.

She tried to remember everything her father had ever taught her about dealing with difficult situations, then she realized that he'd never taught her anything about any situation. She thought about the little stuffed bunny rabbit she used to have when she was a baby. She realized her mind was wandering and she had to get back to the problem at hand.

Candi walked over to the larger dragon.

"You slew this creature?" she asked the first prince.

"Yes."

Candi touched the dragon's head, then quickly drew back her hand. She wiped her fingers on her skirt.

"This dragon is not real," she said. The first prince put his hands in his pockets and began kicking at the dirt.

"Well, sure it's real," he said in a quiet voice.

"It is not. It's made out of wax."

"No, it's real," the prince said, his voice barely more than a whisper.

"Look, the sun is making the edges melt," Candi said.

"Let's divide it into candles!" a voice in the crowd cried out. Within minutes, the wax dragon was split into tiny pieces and carried away.

"I guess I'll be going now," the first prince said, creeping away.

Candi started to approach the smaller dragon, but the second prince stopped her.

"You don't want to look at that up close," he said.

"Why not?" Candi asked.

"Because, uh, dead dragons begin to, uh, smell bad, and I wouldn't want you to, uh, smell anything bad," he replied.

"I'm positive I'd like to see it up close," Candi said firmly. She walked up to the dragon and ran her hand along its body.

"This isn't a dragon!"

"Uh, sure it is," the second prince said.

"Then why is my hand green?" Candi asked, holding up her now-green hand. "It doesn't add up. What is this really?"

"A dragon," the second prince insisted.

Candi touched the dragon's head.

"This is a rubber mask!" she exclaimed.

"Uh, no, it's not," the second prince said.

Candi pulled the rubber mask off.

"This is a sleeping cow that you've painted green and put a mask on," Candi said.

Embarrassed, the second prince disappeared into the crowd, leaving behind the sleeping green cow. It began to snore.

Candi turned to the third prince, who was biting his nails.

"You slew this giant?" Candi asked.

"Sure, yeah," the third prince answered, staring fixedly at his shoes. Candi approached the giant and ran her fingers along it. She checked her hand, and it wasn't covered with wax or green paint.

"Was it an evil giant, terrorizing a town of innocent people?" Candi asked.

"Um, yeah," the third prince said. He still wouldn't look directly at Candi, which was making her suspicious.

"Was there a great battle?" she continued.

The prince's chin began to quiver. "Yes," he whispered.

"You didn't kill this giant, did you?" Candi asked. Big tears started to roll down the prince's cheeks. "Did you?" she repeated.

"Okay, okay, I admit it! I didn't kill it. I bribed it to play dead." The third prince escaped into the crowd, leaving behind the giant, who opened one eye, peered at the crowd, then went back to playing dead.

Candi was extremely, unbelievably, monumentally frustrated.

"Argh!" she cried. She was much too upset to form her thoughts into coherent words. She wandered slowly back to the castle. Just as she was about to climb the stairs to her room, her father appeared.

"Father, my plan did not work," she said. She blinked back

the tears that threatened to spill down her cheeks.

"That's dreadful, er, truly dreadful." The king started to walk away but Candi grabbed his arm.

"Plus I have a green cow to deal with," Candi added, distressed.

"Splendid, splendid," the king said, patting her on the arm. "I'm sure you'll do fine."

Candi went up to her room and sat on her bed. She spied the list she had pinned up on her wall, and it gave her new hope.

Candi read the second item on the list, "Kiss a frog and it will turn into a handsome prince."

III. KISSING FROGS

The next morning, Candi set off to find a frog. She wandered all over the kingdom for three hours until she found a swamp. She knew that a swamp would be unpleasant, but she hadn't expected it to be so smelly and icky and, well, mucky. She wished that she'd thought to put on some boots, and maybe wear something more practical than her full-length gown, but it was too late to worry about that now.

Candi had no idea how to find a frog, much less catch one. "Here, froggie, froggie," she called a couple of times, then whistled, but no frogs appeared. "Souie, souie," she called.

A few wild pigs came running out of the bushes, but no frogs. "Ribbit, ribbit," she called.

A frog appeared.

"You're the most beautiful frog I've ever seen," she declared. It was also the only real frog that Candi had ever seen, but Candi didn't let that stop her from thinking that it was the most beautiful frog in the entire world.

"Ribbit," the frog said, blithely unaware that it was being considered as husband material.

"Come here, you froggie," Candi called softly.

The frog just looked at her sleepily with its big, bulging eyes.

Candi tried to grab the frog, but it hopped out of the way. She tried to throw herself on top of it, but again it hopped out of the way. Candi found herself face-down in the swamp. She picked herself up and, scraping the muck out of her hair, stared at the frog. It stared back at her.

Candi realized she needed some serious frog-catching tools, so she walked back to the castle. She had no idea what these serious frog-catching tools would be, but she didn't let that stop her.

Swamp water oozed between her toes with each step she took. It wasn't entirely unpleasant. She thought it must be similar to walking barefoot in a large, shallow jar of peanut butter.

Once back at the castle, Candi took a long bath and wished with all her might that swamp water didn't smell so incredibly bad. The wishing didn't do any good, but it made Candi feel better. She emerged from the bath in a happier mood and considerably less smelly.

The next morning, Candi set off for the swamp again, fully prepared for frog-catching. She wore gumboots and carried a net. It was her father's net for catching butterflies. She was sure he wouldn't mind that she'd borrowed it.

At the swamp, Candi waited around for a frog to appear. After three hours, she remembered to call, "Ribbit, ribbit."

A frog appeared instantly.

Candi crept up to it. After three tries and two dunks in the swamp, she caught it in the butterfly net. It was much slimier and wigglier than she had expected.

"Eeewww, frog germs. This is yucky. Really yucky," she cried out loud. She leaned over to kiss it, but chickened out. "Bleah. I don't like this one bit."

She took a few deep breaths, gathered up her courage, and closed her eyes— then she planted a big fat kiss on its slimy green head.

Candi waited.

Nothing happened.

She wiped her mouth on her sleeve and waited some more.

Still, nothing happened.

"I'm waiting, froggie," Candi said and, closing her eyes, she kissed it again.

She waited.

Again nothing happened.

"Come on, be a good froggie and turn into a handsome prince," Candi pleaded. "Or even a so-so looking prince." She kissed it a third time and waited.

Still more nothing.

"How odd. Could this be a dud frog?" Candi wondered. She let the frog go and started looking for another one.

"Ribbit, ribbit," she called. Another frog appeared. It sat calmly, completely and totally unaware that it was about to be kissed. Candi snuck up to it and caught it in the butterfly net. It was even greener and bumpier and slimier than the last one—by no means the most beautiful frog in the world—but Candi decided to give it a try. She kissed it on the forehead.

Nothing happened.

"Doubly odd. Another dud frog?" Candi wondered. "This seemed much easier in the fairy tales. And I don't recall reading anything about the frogs being so incredibly slimy and smelly."

She released the frog and caught yet another one. She kissed it and waited.

Something happened this time, but it wasn't what Candi had been expecting. The frog turned into a large yellow canary.

"Tweet," said the canary.

"Right idea, wrong species," Candi said. The canary flew away.

The next frog that Candi kissed turned into a big white bunny. It wriggled its nose at Candi, then hopped out of the swamp and into the forest.

"I'm getting closer, I guess," Candi said, hope growing in her voice. She caught and kissed yet another frog and it turned into a monkey—a monkey that screeched and searched for lice in Candi's hair. *(It didn't find any, of course.)*

Candi's lips were getting chapped by this point. She was cold and wet from falling into the swamp, though her feet were rather comfortable in the gumboots. So comfortable, in fact, that Candi thought she might wear them all the time. She decided to try kissing one more frog before she went home.

"Come here you stupid-slimy-smelly-lumpy-bumpy-mean-green-excuse-for-an-amphibian," she called out crossly.

Naturally, no frogs appeared. "Ribbit, ribbit," she called. A frog hopped up to her. Candi bent her poor, tired, chapped lips down to the frog and kissed it.

Poof!

Before Candi stood a breathtakingly handsome prince.

"You are breathtakingly handsome," she told him.

"I know," he replied as he pulled a small mirror out of his pocket and checked his reflection. "I am quite magnificent, am I not?"

"Well, yes," Candi said.

"Am I not the most dashingly handsome, strikingly charming, just downright good-looking guy you've ever seen?" the prince continued.

"I guess so," Candi said, as a small frown crept across her face.

"Go on, you can do better than that, tell me how great you think I am," the prince urged as he checked his teeth in the mirror. "I just know you think I'm wonderful."

"Don't you want to know anything about me? Wouldn't you like to talk about me?" Candi asked.

"Why would I, when I could be talking about myself?" the prince asked as he smoothed his hair.

"I liked you better when you were a frog," Candi said, but the prince didn't hear her. He was too busy admiring his reflection to notice anything else. Candi left him preening in the swamp and returned to the castle. Cold, tired, wet, frustrated, and increasingly discouraged, she checked the third item on her list of ways to find a husband.

"Eat a poisoned apple, fall into a deep sleep, and wait for the kiss of a handsome prince to wake you up," Candi read. Exhausted, she fell asleep in her dirty clothes and gumboots, on top of her quilt. Her lips were still chapped from all that frog-kissing, and her hands were covered with frog slime.

IV. GETTING SICK

Candi woke up the next morning dirty and smelly. She took a long bath and wished with all her might to find a prince who was nice. She didn't even care about handsome anymore, as long as he was nice. And maybe noticed she was alive.

Candi reread number three on the list of ways to find a husband. Upon reflection, poison didn't seem like such a good idea. Poison killed people, or at least made them very, very sick.

"I don't want to be very, very sick," Candi said. "Maybe I'll just make myself a tiny bit sick, with something other than poison, and see if that's enough to find a prince." She dug around in the castle's many closets until she found her father's hidden stash of Halloween candy. He had always warned Candi that too much candy would make her sick— but that was exactly what Candi wanted.

She ate everything in the bag—chocolates, potato chips, suckers, caramels, hard candies, soft candies, chewy candies, ooey-gooey-good candies. Everything.

Very quickly, Candi started to feel not very good.

In fact, within a very short time, she began to feel downright lousy.

"Ooooooh," she moaned. "Will my prince appear now?"

Within an even shorter time, Candi felt extremely ill.

"Oooooh," she moaned again. She clutched at her stomach, then fainted.

The next thing Candi knew, she was in her own bed and a so-so looking man was leaning over her.

"Are you my so-so looking prince, come to rescue me?" Candi asked as she reached up and planted a big juicy kiss on the man's lips.

"I'm a doctor," he said, surprised.

"Wow! My husband is a prince and a doctor!" Candi exclaimed.

"You don't understand," the doctor said. "I've come to help you get better. You've been sick all afternoon."

"You're sure you're not my so-so looking prince?" Candi asked.

"I know I'm so-so looking, but I'm definitely not a prince," the doctor said.

"This is not working out at all the way I thought it would," Candi said in a very small voice. The doctor patted her on the hand.

"You'll be fine. You'll just have a tummyache for a while. What were you eating?"

"All the Halloween candy I could find."

"You should have known that would make you sick," the doctor said.

"But I wanted to get sick and fall into a deep sleep."

"Oh," the doctor said wisely, "trying to find a husband, are you?"

"Yes," Candi replied.

"Let me give you some advice," the doctor said. "Getting sick and throwing up on someone won't make him your prince."

"Is that so?" replied Candi, then she threw up on the doctor.

He left in a big hurry.

Candi was alone—alone and unbelievably frustrated.

"Argh!" she yelled. "I've reached a new level of frustration! All my previous frustration was just a rehearsal for this new, incredibly high level of frustration!"

Candi grabbed a math book and spent a few hours doing mathematical problems, until she felt calm and relaxed. Then she grabbed her list and read the final method of finding a husband on it.

"Find a fairy godmother." That sounded better than the other options—all of which had failed miserably—but how did one go about finding a fairy godmother?

V. LOOKING FOR MAGIC

Candi paced around her room. "How am I going to find a fairy godmother?" she repeated over and over to herself.

Candi knew that a fairy godmother was a magic creature. The only person Candi could think of who could perform magic was the wizard who had turned her mother into a pickle. Candi certainly didn't have any fond feelings for that wizard, but she didn't know who else to turn to. She was down to the last method on her list. She needed some magic and she needed it fast. So she set off to find the wizard.

He wasn't hard to find.

You see, times were tough for the wizard. He had been quite successful at one time. He had toured the kingdom performing magical and mathematical feats.

The wizard had been known far and wide as a genius, faster with numbers and calculations than any other living being. But then came the fateful poker game with the king, in which the wizard had lost *(among other things)* his watch. And what good is a wizard without a watch?

Not much.

The wizard no longer knew what time it was, so he kept sleeping in and missing his engagements to perform magic. People quickly grew unhappy with him. "How can he be any good with numbers, if he doesn't even know what time it is?" they said.

The wizard became so poor that he had to advertise his magic on posters in the streets. It was one of these posters that Candi found, and the poster directed her to the wizard's house.

Candi knocked on the door. There was no answer. Candi knocked again, then a third time.

"Go away! I'm not buying anything!" a gruff voice yelled from inside the house.

"But I'm not selling anything," Candi said. The door opened, just a crack.

"You're not?" the voice asked, less gruffly.

"No," Candi said. "I'm here to buy some magic, if you're the wizard, that is." The door was flung wide open and a small man with a wide grin pulled Candi into the house.

"Really? You're here to buy magic? You're not just kidding around, are you?" the wizard asked, hopping impatiently from one foot to the other.

Candi began to think he was definitely odd.

"You are the wizard?" she asked.

"Of course, of course! The wizard—that's me!" he exclaimed, then spun around in circles with joy.

"What kind of magic would you like? Something fancy?" He inspected Candi's fine clothes. "You look rich, with that fancy dress, although I don't understand why you're wearing gumboots. No matter, no matter! If you wear gumboots and you want magic, you're wonderful to me!"

Candi had absolutely no doubts now—the wizard was odd. Yup, she was sure of it.

The wizard grabbed Candi's hand and planted a big wet kiss on it, then he kissed his own hands. "Whee! Someone wants my magic!" he cried, dancing around the room. Suddenly he became very subdued and gentlemanly. "Where are my manners? I am Wally, the Wacky, Wonderful Wizard. And what is your name, my dear?"

"Princess Candi," she replied, relieved that Wally had come to his senses at last.

"I beg your pardon?" Wally asked. His face went white and his big grin disappeared. "Did you say Princess Candi?"

"Yes," Candi said. Wally's face turned purple.

"Princess Candi, daughter of the king?"

"Yes, that's me."

"Get out!" Wally screamed.

Candi was shocked. "Why?" she finally managed to ask.

"Get out!" Wally screamed again. "Your family has taken enough from me already!"

"But I need your magic."

"I'd rather drink snot and eat boogers," Wally said.

"Is there no way you'll help me?" Candi asked.

"Not that I can see. No!" Wally shouted, shoving Candi toward the door.

Candi thought and thought and thought some more, as quickly as she could, desperate to find a way to get Wally to help her. Just as Candi was being pushed out the door, she thought of a way.

"Wait!" she cried, clinging to Wally's arm. "What if I challenge you to a game, a contest?"

Despite himself, Wally was interested.

"What kind of contest?" he asked.

"A mathematical one," Candi said.

Wally laughed and laughed and laughed some more, until he was laughing so hard he had to sit down. Tears rolled down his cheeks from laughing so hard.

"You challenge me to a math contest?" he finally sputtered, then laughed for three more minutes.

"Yes," Candi answered calmly.

"Don't waste my time," Wally said.

"I'm quite serious," Candi said.

Wally stared at her.

"And if you win," Wally began, but he broke into uproarious laughter again. Candi had to wait another three minutes for Wally to regain his composure. "And if you win," he repeated, chuckling, "what do you get?"

"I get a fairy godmother," Candi said.

"That's easy enough," Wally agreed.

A new thought occurred to Candi. If she had been a made-up character, rather than a real person, a light bulb would have appeared above her head.

"...and, I get my mother turned back into a person," she said.

"I suppose you don't want your father to be a goof anymore, either," Wally said, sighing.

"He's a goof?"

"This is going to be ridiculously easy."

"What do you want, if you win?" Candi asked.

Wally thought for a long while before answering. "Chickie-poo, I want to turn you into a pickle."

VI. THE CONTEST

The idea of being a pickle didn't appeal much to Candi. In fact, Candi thought it was a hideous idea. Her mother was a pickle, and her mother's life seemed pretty darned boring. Besides, Candi had never looked good in green. "How about I just give you my gumboots?"

"No. I want to turn you into a pickle," Wally said.

"Hmmm, that would multiply the problem," said Candi. "But okay." What choice did she have?

Wally rubbed his hands together with glee. "Let's get started!"

Wally and Candi agreed to ask each other math questions until one of them was stumped. Whomever was stumped first would be the loser.

"What is the square root of 49?" Candi asked.

"That's too easy," Wally said, smirking. "Seven. What is the square root of 81?"

"Nine." Candi smiled.

Wally looked surprised that Candi actually knew the answer.

"What is the square root of 196?" Candi asked.

Wally had to think for a few moments before answering. "Fourteen. Now what is the square root of 205?" he asked slyly.

"You're trying to trick me. There is no even square root of 205," Candi said.

Wally was so impressed by Candi's math skills that he was starting to get worried. Was it possible? Could he actually lose in a math contest? The thought had never occurred to him before.

"I'm tired of square roots," Candi said. "Let's try something different. If I have ten apples and I give away all but three, how many apples do I have left?"

"Seven," Wally said without thinking. His entire being was consumed by the thought of losing, by how absolutely hideously repulsive and altogether icky that would be.

"Pardon?" Candi asked.

"Seven," Wally repeated, then he realized his mistake. "I mean three! I said three!"

"You said seven! Twice!" Candi shouted triumphantly while Wally pouted. "You're wrong. You're wrong! And you know you're wrong!" Candi gloated, which made Wally pout more. "Now perform some magic!"

"Couldn't I just give you some new gumboots and we'll call it even?" Wally mumbled.

"No."

"Best two out of three?"

"I want a fairy godmother. I want my mother not to be a pickle. I want my father not to be goofy, and I want all three right now!"

"Fine," Wally said, still pouting.

VII. THE FAIRY GODMOTHER

Candi found herself instantly back in her own room in the castle.

"That's just fine and dandy," she said, "but where's my fairy godmother?"

Suddenly, out of nowhere, a withered old woman appeared in the room beside Candi.

"Where did you come from?" Candi exclaimed.

"Out of nowhere," the withered old woman said.

"That figures," said Candi. As she was pondering this bit of information, a new thought occurred to her. "Why are you here?"

"To help you find a husband."

"How did you know I'm looking for a husband?"

"We fairy godmothers just know."

"Are you a fairy godmother?"

"You're a quick one, aren't you? You make that Cinderella chick look like a real brain surgeon."

"Which one is Cinderella again?" Candi asked.

"Read the book," the fairy godmother replied, rolling her eyes and pointing at the collection of fairy tales that lay discarded on the floor. "Let's get this show on the road. I'm a busy woman. So how do you want your prince? Tall? Dark? Handsome? No visible scars?"

"You mean you can just order one up for me? Right here and now?"

"Sure can. Just tell me what you want, and make it snappy."

"Well," Candi said, "make him a perfect prince, then."

"Perfect," the fairy godmother muttered to herself. "No pressure, no pressure, just perfection."

Poof!

Before Candi stood a prince who was, well, perfect. He was handsome, but not so handsome as to look phony. He was tall, but not so tall as to tower above Candi. He had perfect teeth, but not so perfect that they looked like dentures. He smelled vaguely of strawberries and puppies and warm summer days. The prince took one look at Candi and fell to his knees before her.

"My darling!" he cried as he grabbed one of Candi's hands and kissed it. "My princess, my beautiful princess. I love you and adore you." He grabbed Candi's other hand and kissed it. "How perfectly happy we will be, together for the rest of our perfect lives."

The fairy godmother smiled as she inspected the prince. "I guess my work is done," she said.

"I want to know everything about you," said the perfect prince. "I want to know what your favorite color is and how many lumps of sugar you take in your tea and how you got this perfect little freckle on your perfect little wrist."

Candi felt relieved. "I'll show you around the castle," she told the prince. "We can talk. You can meet my parents, and I'll show you my collection of math books. Maybe we could even solve some math problems together later."

"Don't be silly!" the prince cried, as he continued to shower praise and kisses upon Candi. "I have no interest in math. I'm only interested in making you deliriously happy every minute of every day."

A small frown crossed Candi's face. "You don't like math?"

"Math is boring," the prince said. "I don't want to do anything boring ever again. I just want to love and adore you all day long."

"Um, Fairy Godmother?" Candi called. "Wait!"

"What's the problem?" the fairy godmother snapped.

"Is this all the perfect prince does?"

The perfect prince paused long enough to look affronted. "I have slain both a dragon and a giant. I have kissed an enchanted princess back to life, and I've even spent a summer as a frog," he said, then he resumed kissing Candi's hands.

"You asked for a perfect man, so I gave you a perfect man! Look at him, groveling at your feet. What more could you ask for?" the fairy godmother shrieked.

"He's kind of boring," Candi said slowly.

The fairy godmother looked incredulous. "A perfect man groveling at your feet is boring?"

"He doesn't like to do math problems," Candi said. "Plus, where's the romance and falling-in-love part?"

"What do you need all that junk for?"

"It's fun," Candi said. She thought about everything that had happened to her recently and everything she had learned from her experiences. She thought for so long that the fairy godmother started making shadow puppets on the wall to entertain herself. The prince, meanwhile, was kissing Candi's hands and going on and on about "perfect woman" and "happy forever" and other such nonsense.

Finally, Candi reached a decision. "All things being equal, I want to find a husband on my own," she said. "I don't want to use magic. Any 'magic' that happens between my prince and me will be created by us, not by someone else." Candi skipped off downstairs, happy with her decision.

The fairy godmother disappeared in a puff of smoke, taking the perfect prince with her.

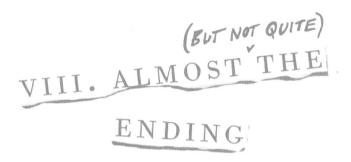

VIII. ALMOST THE (BUT NOT QUITE) ENDING

Candi reached the bottom of the stairs to discover her father and mother happily embracing. At least Candi assumed it was her mother—Candi had only ever known her as a pickle in a jar.

"Candi!" the king cried when he saw his daughter. "My darling Candi! It's amazing. It's magic. Come and meet your mother!" Candi noticed that the king was carrying a book—a book with words in it, not just pictures—and that he had actually called her by her proper name. Candi hugged her parents.

IX. THE ENDING
OF COURSE!

Candi and her mother got to know each other and grew to love each other. Candi's mother was far more interesting, now that she was no longer a pickle.

The king stopped being such a goof, and he and Candi had numerous deep, meaningful conversations. They read books together and the king became quite skilled at mathematical problems.

Wally became a successful magician and mathematician again, after Candi presented him with a watch that kept perfect time. She didn't know about the watch that Wally had lost all those years ago, but she thought that a handsome gold watch would make him feel better after losing the math contest. Which it did, of course.

And what about Candi's search for a prince? Well, Candi and her now-intelligent father and her non-pickle mother all agreed that Candi was too young to get married, so Candi went off to university on a math scholarship. She had a wonderful time there, learning new things every day and meeting all kinds of wonderful and interesting people.

One day, as she was talking to her friend Prince Jack *(who was also a math student and had the rare talent of being able to balance a spoon on his nose)*, she experienced a strange feeling.

"My goodness," she said. "I do feel strange, to the nth degree. I feel all warm and gushy inside."

"Does it feel like there's cotton in your mouth?" Jack asked.

"Yes," Candi replied, "and tingles in my hands and jelly in my legs and—"

"—butterflies in your stomach and squirrels in your elbows," Jack finished.

"Yes."

"Me too."

Candi and Jack stared deeply into each other's eyes. It didn't take them long *(well, not longer than an hour or two, anyway)* to realize that they were wildly, passionately, deeply in love. It was pure chemistry. They were married a year later.

Everyone lived happily ever after, for as long as they could.

But you knew it would all work out in the end, *didn't you?*

THE END

ABOUT
the
AUTHOR

SHERI RADFORD is the editor of two visitor magazines and spends her days wrestling with commas, taming adjectives, and banishing adverbs. As the author of several silly, award-winning books for children, she spends her evenings playing, imagining, and creating. Sheri lives in Vancouver with her messy husband and two even messier cats.

ABOUT
the
ILLUSTRATOR

QIN LENG is a designer and animator based in Toronto, Canada. She has received many awards for her animated short films and artworks and has worked at the National Film Board of Canada in Montreal and CORE digital pictures and Yowza Animation in Toronto.